U0111309

Our Chinese Hometown

A Hungry Tiger in the Kitchen

Written by **Ada Ho How-sim**
Illustrated by **Sheung Wong**

Sun Ya Publications (HK) Ltd.
www.sunya.com.hk

Fun China

Our Chinese Hometown: A Hungry Tiger in the Kitchen

Author
Ada Ho How-sim

Illustrator
Sheung Wong

Reviewer
Judith Malmsbury

Executive Editor
Tracy Wong

Graphic Designer
Karla Lau

Publisher
Sun Ya Publications (HK) Ltd.
18/F, North Point Industrial Building, 499 King's Road, Hong Kong
Tel: (852) 2138 7998 Fax: (852) 2597 4003
Website: https://www.sunya.com.hk
E-mail: marketing@sunya.com.hk

Distributor
SUP Publishing Logistics (HK) Ltd.
16/F, Tsuen Wan Industrial Centre, 220-248 Texaco Road,
Tsuen Wan, N.T., Hong Kong
Tel: (852) 2150 2100 Fax: (852) 2407 3062
E-mail: info@suplogistics.com.hk

Printer
C & C Offset Printing Co., Ltd.
36 Ting Lai Road, Tai Po, N.T., Hong Kong

Edition
First Published in August 2024

All rights reserved.

ISBN: 978-962-08-8445-0
© 2024 Sun Ya Publications (HK) Ltd.
18/F, North Point Industrial Building, 499 King's Road, Hong Kong
Published in Hong Kong SAR, China
Printed in China

About the Story

Evan Wong's grandma is very confused. Recently, food in the kitchen has been disappearing for no reason. Could it be that a tiger stole it?

There is indeed a "Siberian tiger*" in the Wongs' home, someone Evan loves very much.

* In China, the Siberian tiger is also called the "Northeast tiger".

"Strange, so strange! I clearly placed food here. It's missing again. How come?"

Evan's grandma keeps looking around in the kitchen.

What is Grandma looking for?

Last month, a friend sent some pork jerky to Grandma. She put it in the kitchen cabinet, but now she cannot find it anywhere.

Last week, there was a box of fried chicken in the fridge, but only two or three pieces were left the next day. The rest were gone!

Strange, so strange!

Except for Grandma, nobody seems to mind why the food is mysteriously missing.

Evan's father comforts Grandma, "Maybe a tiger has sneaked into our kitchen."

"What? A tiger?" Grandma asks. She frowns and sighs, "We live on the 20th floor!"

"Maybe it's a tiger that knows how to take a lift!"
Evan's mother smiles and teases.

A tiger riding in a lift? How funny! Evan cannot
help laughing.

Do tigers know how to take a lift? Maybe! We don't know. However, Evan does have a "tiger" in his family, and it is a famous "Siberian tiger".

Evan's grandpa was born in the Year of the Tiger in Heilongjiang province*. The province has "dragon" in its name. Both a tiger and a dragon. Bravo, Grandpa!

He even has a nickname — "Siberian Tiger" — given by his friends. Grandpa likes it a lot!

*Heilongjiang (黑龍江) is a province in the far northeast part of China. In Chinese, its name means "black dragon river".

Grandpa loves telling Evan stories about tigers.

"Evan, look, the tiger's head is big and round. There are three black horizontal stripes and one vertical strip on its forehead. The stripes make the Chinese character '王*', meaning 'king'!"

"The tiger king!" Evan exclaims.

"Oh yes, '王' is also our family name. Ha ha..."

* Spelled Wong or Wang, the Chinese character "王" is a common family name in China.

9

Evan holds Grandpa's big, round face in his hands.
He counts carefully, "One, two, three, four, and five."
"Grandpa, you have five lines on your forehead. You are
more powerful than a tiger."
"Ha ha, ha ha...", Grandpa laughs and slides off the sofa
onto the floor.

Grandma returns from grocery shopping.

As soon as she opens the door, she complains, "Grandpa, your tiger voice is really loud. Even the security guard on the ground floor hears your laughter."

Grandpa makes a face,
"Shh... Let's be quiet, Evan."

Siberian tigers are the largest tigers in the world. They are the "King of Tigers".

Grandpa is 190 cm tall and weighs 95 kg. He is definitely a big guy.

Ever since Evan was in kindergarten, Grandpa has been picking him up from school every day. From far away little Evan can see Grandpa among all the parents. Together, they stride back home hand in hand.

Grandpa has a lot of friends.
   As they walk along the street, they see different neighbours.

They laugh and chat about everything under the sun.

It is just a 10-minute walk from
school to home.
    Sometimes, it takes Grandpa and
Evan almost an hour to get home.

Grandma can't help grumbling, "I've been waiting for both of you for ages. I am so worried!"

"Honey, I'm sorry. We met some friends..." Grandpa scratches his grey hair.

"I promise! I'll call and let you know next time," he continues.

Siberian tigers are not afraid of cold weather. They come and go freely in a world of ice and snow.

Grandpa is not afraid of cold weather either.

When Grandma asks him to put on more clothes and keep warm in winter, he frowns and says, "Winter in Hong Kong is nothing to me!"

Grandpa continues speaking. "In Heilongjiang, winter temperatures may be as low as -30℃."

In the winter in Heilongjiang, everyone is wrapped warmly from head to toe.

Parents always warn their children, "Be careful! Don't let the icy wind blow your ears away."

Siberian tigers become very active when the white snow gleams and shines.

Grandpa is enthusiastic. He opens his round eyes and roars, "Oow, ow..."

Evan pretends to be a little tiger, riding on Grandpa's back, "Oow, ow...Oow, ow..."

The two "Siberian tigers" are crawling and roaring around the house.

Grandma sighs, "Hey, be careful! You two tigers, don't break the vase!"

"Yes, ma'am!" Grandpa says. He makes a face and says to Evan, "We tigers are going to have some reading time!"

These past few months, Grandpa has no longer played tiger riding with Evan.

Grandpa, who used to walk with long strides, is slowing down.

Even if he does not run into his friends, it takes him half an hour to walk from school to home.

Sometimes, he is even a little out of breath.

In the wild, Siberian tigers are agile. They are excellent hunters by birth.

Also, they need a lot of food. A Siberian tiger eats more than 10 kg of meat each day. That is almost 4,000 kg of meat in a year!

Evan touches Grandpa's big belly and says, "No wonder Grandpa also likes to eat big chunks of meat."

Grandma overhears Evan's words in the kitchen.

She says, "The doctor said Grandpa needs to lose weight! He should eat less meat from now on."

Grandpa is not at all concerned.

He gives a thumbs up to Grandma, "You know, the food you cook is too delicious to resist."

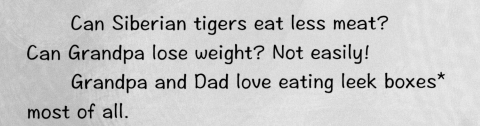

Can Siberian tigers eat less meat?
Can Grandpa lose weight? Not easily!
    Grandpa and Dad love eating leek boxes*
most of all.

However, Grandma takes away the leek boxes from Grandpa.

Then, she places a bowl of millet congee[+] in front of him and says, "Millet congee is good for your health. Eat more of it!"

"Alas! Eat millet congee for dinner? What kind of a tiger am I?" Grandpa protests helplessly.

*Leek boxes (韭菜盒子) are a type of Chinese traditional snack popular in the northern part of China. They are small pocket pies filled with leeks, fried eggs and other savoury ingredients.

[+]Millet congee (小米粥) is like oatmeal porridge.

The weather suddenly turned cold last night.
Grandma brings out a dish of pork and pickled cabbage.
The sour cabbage together with the fat, smooth pork
belly is so mouth-watering!

Grandma picks out some vegetables, fungi and tofu.
    She puts them in a bowl and gives it to Grandpa, "Eat these. These are very healthy."

Grandpa shakes his head as he asks, "Alas! Have you ever seen a Siberian tiger eating tofu?"

Today, Grandma has been searching in the
kitchen for a long time.
  She asks with a puzzled look, "There was
for sure a large pot of stewed pork belly with
glass noodles* in the fridge. How could it be
gone now?"

*Stewed pork belly with glass
  noodles (豬肉燉粉條) is a
  popular dish in northeastern
  China. It tastes soft and juicy.
  Every family has its own
  recipe.

Evan's mum smiles
and says, "Grandma, a
Siberian tiger sneaked
into our kitchen late
last night!"

Dad blinks and
adds, "A very, very
hungry Siberian tiger!"

Acting as if nothing happened, Grandpa keeps calm and cool.

Then he says, "Told you. Siberian tigers are not vegetarians!"

"Ha ha...", the whole family bursts into laughter.

Evan hugs and kisses Grandpa.
Whether vegetarian or meat-eating, Grandpa is the "tiger" Evan loves the most.

Notes to parents

China has a vast territory. The unique features of each local environment give special characteristics to its people. There are many differences between the southern and northern regions of China in terms of climate, diet, natural environment, and even people's body shapes. Hong Kong is a coastal city in southern China, while Heilongjiang is the northern-most province in China. The people of these two places have completely different lifestyles.

The story refers to a traditional family structure where three generations – grandparents, parents and child – live together under the same roof. The unique characteristics of people from northeast China can be found in the story. Readers can also experience a deep affection between the older generation and the young, as well as the joy and harmony of the family. Let's cherish the traditional virtue of respecting the older generation and caring for the young.

At the end of the book is a suggested activity. Children can explore the customs of their hometowns and enrich their understanding of their own families.

Discovering the Traditions of Your Hometown

Hey, kids! Do you know where your hometown is? How about your parents' hometowns? How much do you know about them? Let's ask the members of your family the following questions to learn about the customs and traditions of their hometowns.

1. Where is your hometown?

   _____

2. Does your hometown have any special customs or traditions?

   _____

3. What kind of food is unique to your hometown?

   _____

4. Do you know any famous people from your hometown?

   _____

You can ask more questions and write down the answers in a notebook. You can also look for photos online or draw pictures of famous places and special things in the hometowns. Put all the information together and make your own booklet about your own hometown and family members' hometowns. Then, share it with your friends!

About the Author
Ada Ho How-sim

Ada Ho is an Honorary Fellow of The Education University of Hong Kong. She holds a master's degree in Education from Macquarie University, Australia. She is a former principal and currently works as a writer, school director and guest lecturer at The Education University of Hong Kong.

In addition to her educational roles, Ada has held various public service positions, including school manager positions in different schools. She has also served as a professional consultant on literature and arts for the Leisure and Cultural Services Department of Hong Kong. She was also the former president of the Hong Kong Children's Literature Association.

Ada is committed to promoting children's reading and possesses a profound understanding of and concern for children's growth and development. As of 2024, she has published more than 180 books.

About the Illustrator

Sheung Wong

Sheung Wong is a talented illustrator from Hong Kong. Despite being born deaf, her passion for drawing has been with her since childhood. Graduating with a master's degree in Printmaking from the Guangzhou Academy of Fine Arts, Sheung combines printmaking, and pencil and chalk textures with digital techniques. She has been creating illustrations for various companies and publishers since 2014.